"I have never forgotten that winter. The long evenings of reading and study in our warm rooms (and) looking forward to my visits to Paris with Gertrude and Alice."

Fritz Peters

This story is loosely based on a chapter in **BOYHOOD WITH GURDJIEFF**, a memoir written by Fritz Peters.

Thank you to:

Bruce Kellner for his sage advice and encouragement, and all the other GertrudeandAlice fans who have been awaiting this book.

Kathleen Gross for her beautiful book design.

Betsy Nolan for her just knowing this book would get done!

Catherine Peters and Richard L. Weaver (Tale Weaver Publishing) for their support of this work.

And to Vishwa Marwah who has journeyed with me on our GertrudeandAlice adventures, always being the there there.
–Hans Gallas

This book is dedicated to Julius and Loretta.
–Tom Hachtman

Book design by Kathleen Gross, StudioKG, San Francisco

Copyright ©2011 by Hans Gallas and Tom Hachtman
First Edition
Printed by Tien Wah Press (PTE) Limited, Singapore
10 9 8 7 6 5 4 3 2 1

For more information, visit gertrudeandalice.com/fritzandtom

ISBN 978-0-615-51450-5

GertrudeandAlice
Editions
A ROSE IS A ROSE IS A ROSE IS A ROSE IS A ROSE IS A...

Gertrude and Alice and Fritz and Tom

An Artful Adventure with Gertrude Stein and Alice B. Toklas

by Hans Gallas

Illustrations by Tom Hachtman

*O*nce there were two amusing American ladies, Gertrude Stein and Alice B. Toklas.

They lived in a mighty marvelous apartment in Paris, which was filled with masterful modern paintings that covered the walls, floor to ceiling.

Gertrude was a really remarkable writer and sometimes Alice called her "Lovey."

Alice was a constantly creative cook and sometimes Gertrude called her "Pussy."

*P*icasso was one of their favorite famous artists whose masterful modern paintings hung floor to ceiling.

Gertrude and Alice thought his positively pleasing portrait of Gertrude was precious.

One day at teatime, a letter arrived from a treasured trusted friend:

"Dear Gertrude and Alice,
Will you baby-sit my beautifully
behaved boys, Fritz and Tom,
over Thanksgiving?
            Sincerely,
                    Jane"

Gertrude and Alice thought children were basically beautifully behaved too, and they liked to baby-sit, but they had a few quite quirky questions.

"There, there," said Gertrude, "What to do? What to do? What to do?"

"Lovey," said Alice, "I've heard Fritz and Tom can be a horrible handful. They play pesky pranks at school and are not fond of challenging chores."

"*H*orrible handful? Pussy, you mean beastly brats who play pesky pranks and are not fond of challenging chores?

How beastly can the brats be? We have two dogs, Basket and Pépé.

Rose is a rose is a rose is a rose."

Alice made a fiercely funny face and dropped her tasteful turquoise teacup.

Gertrude finished her tepid Tibetan tea and five of Alice's truly tasty teacakes.

They decided that Fritz and Tom could visit after all.

The beastly boys arrived on Thanksgiving and rang the doorbell.

A second floor window opened.

"Fritz and Tom? Happy Thanksgiving," shouted Gertrude. "Here is the key. Alice is creatively cooking in the kitchen. Come in, make yourselves at home. I must take my belated bubble bath!"

She threw the key out the window.

"We must be early," said Tom.

"Or she must be late," said Fritz, turning the key in the door.

"What a strangely stylish salon," said Fritz, looking around.

"Look at this really rambling room!" whispered Tom. "There are masterful modern paintings floor to ceiling! It looks like a museum! I hate museums, everything in a museum is musty and moldy."

*F*ritz pressed his nose against one of the paintings.

"This person has four flaming eyes and three thick ears and is not musty and moldy!"

"Hello boys, Happy Thanksgiving," said Alice.

"Please don't press your nose against that positively pleasing painting."

"Come into the dining room instead, and set the table by order of Miss Gertrude Stein, who is finishing her belated bubble bath."

"Ugh, a challenging chore," said Fritz, putting his hand into his pocket.

"Ugh, a challenging chore," said Tom, crossing his arms.

*B*ut Fritz and Tom set the huge heavy table with all of the huge heavy glasses and huge heavy plates and huge heavy silverware.

"*A*merican boys must have an American Thanksgiving!" shouted Gertrude as she strolled into the room.

"*W*ith tantalizingly tasty turkey and perfect pumpkin pie!"

"*I* love crunchy cranberry sauce," said Fritz.

"I love perfect pumpkin pie," said Tom.

"I love tantalizingly tasty turkey," said Alice.

"And I almost forgot the simply scrumptious stuffing with chestnuts and mushrooms and oysters," added Gertrude.

"We ordered these mighty morsels from America for all of us," said Gertrude.

"Wow!" said Fritz.

"Wow! Wow!" said Tom.

"Happy Thanksgiving!" they all said and finished eating Alice's fancy festive feast.

"Afterwards," said Gertrude, "Fritz, you wash the dishes and Tom, you dry the dishes before it's bedtime."

Alice dropped her huge heavy knife in sudden surprise.

"Pussy," said Gertrude the next morning. "Today the boys will learn about Paris. Here is my precise perfect plan."

Alice looked at the precise perfect plan and murmured: "Quite a precise perfect plan. Here is my major must-have map."

Off they went in their carefully cared-for car.

Gertrude was the driver. Fritz sat next to her. Alice and Tom sat in the backseat.

"You press the horn when I say **NOW**," said Gertrude to Fritz.

"First stop, the Eiffel Tower!" shouted Alice, pointing at the major must-have map on her lap.

"WOW!" said Fritz and Tom at the elegantly elevated Eiffel Tower.

They all stood in front of the elegantly elevated Eiffel Tower, and Gertrude asked a tall tanned tourist from Tasmania to take their picture.

"Next stop is King Louis's lovely Louvre museum where you'll see handsome hallowed halls of amazing art very different from the awfully amazing art on our walls," explained Gertrude.

"Ugh, a museum," whispered Tom.

"Ugh, so much walking," whispered Fritz.

"Wasn't that an exceedingly exciting excursion?" said Gertrude three hours later.

"Hmmm?" said Fritz and Tom, rubbing their feet.

"Now to the fabulous famous cathedral, Notre Dame," said Gertrude, and Fritz pressed the horn.

"**Now** not **NOW**," said Gertrude smiling (sort of!)

At Notre Dame, Fritz and Tom climbed the one hundred seventy seven steep steps of the truly tall tower.

*F*ritz took a scarlet silk scarf out of his pocket which Gertrude had given him to wave as a signal when they reached the top of the tower. He waved it at Gertrude and Alice who were sitting in the car.

"They look like ants," said Tom.

"One fat ant and one skinny ant!" said Fritz laughing.

"I wish they were our aunts," said Tom.

"Me too," said Fritz.

Soon Gertrude's precise perfect plan was finished. They had visited many popular Parisian places. It was time for Fritz and Tom to end their truly terrific Thanksgiving visit.

One morning while Alice was fixing more not-yet-tepid Tibetan tea while waiting for Gertrude to finish another belated bubble bath, she found the scarlet silk scarf. It was behind the tasteful turquoise teapot that had only one cup and saucer.

Wrapped in the scarlet silk scarf was a note:

"Dear Miss Stein and
Miss Toklas,

How are you? We are fine. We will
always remember our totally
terrific time in Paris with you.
No more pesky pranks at school
for us, and challenging chores are
now fun.

Your friends,
Fritz and Tom

P.S. May I drive your carefully
cared-for car sometime?
Fritz

P.S.S.
Will you be our amusing
American aunts?"

Alice ran to show Gertrude
the note.

"*P*ussy, don't drop it in the tub," said Gertrude. "This is one of the nicest notes we have ever received."

"Lovey, it is positively pleasing, and I think we would make two amusing American aunts," said Alice B. Toklas.

"Now finish your belated bubble bath, you have some really remarkable writing to do!"

"And you have some constantly creative cooking to do!" said Gertrude Stein.

Who is who is who is who...?

Gertrude Stein (1874-1946) was an American writer who lived in Paris. She and her brothers collected paintings by artists like Picasso and Matisse and invited people to their homes to see the pictures. She wrote many books including one for children called **The World is Round.** She is famous for some of the phrases she wrote such as "Rose is a rose is a rose is a rose," and "There is no there there."

She lived with her partner, Alice B. Toklas, for almost 40 years.

Alice B. Toklas (1877-1967) was born in San Francisco and moved to Paris where she met Gertrude Stein. She was a very good cook and wrote a cook book which has stories about her life with Gertrude and the recipes that she cooked. She also typed the many things that Gertrude wrote.

The "B" in her name is for Babette.

Gertrude did not have a middle name.

Fritz and Tom Peters were American brothers who lived in Paris with their aunt who knew Gertrude and Alice. They went to a boarding school near Paris and would come to visit Gertrude and Alice.

When Fritz was older, he became a writer and wrote a book which had a story about the times he and Tom came to visit Gertrude and Alice.

This book tells about some of their adventures with Gertrude and Alice.

Basket and Pépé
were the dogs of Gertrude and Alice. Basket was a white French poodle and Pépé was a brown chihuahua.

Alice gave Basket his name because she hoped he would carry a basket of flowers in his mouth. Pépé got his name because a chihuahua is a Mexican dog and Pépé is a short Mexican name. (For awhile they had another chihuahua, Byron, named after the English poet.) There were also two Baskets – Basket I and Basket II.

When Gertrude and Alice took walks with the dogs, children wanted to play with them.

Hans Gallas (1949 -) who
wrote this book, was born in Berlin, Germany and grew up in Springfield, Il, the Land of Lincoln.

He has a collection of books, letters, pictures, and lots of other stuff about Gertrude and Alice.

He even made a Gertrude and an Alice puppet because he likes puppets and could not find any of them.

He lives in San Francisco with his longtime partner, Vishwa. They also have a dog named Fritz who doesn't know anything about Gertrude and Alice, but would probably like to chase Basket and Pépé.

Tom Hachtman (aka Mickey Hackman) (1948 -)
who illustrated this book has had pieces in *Mad Magazine, The New Yorker, Playboy, Rolling Stone, Barron's, the Soho News* and the editorial page of the *New York Daily News.*

He is the author/illustrator of **Gertrude's Follies** (St. Martin's Press) based on the comic strip he created in the Soho News. His book, **Double Takes** (Harmony Crown) includes a portrait of "Gertrude Steinem."

Pieces from both books were included in the exhibit "Seeing Gertrude Stein" at the Contemporary Jewish Museum in San Francisco and the National Portrait Gallery, Washington, DC in 2011. Drawings from this book were also shown at the Stanford in Washington (DC) Art Gallery.

The End